'Tis the good reader
that makes the good book.

—Ralph Waldo Emerson

This book is dedicated to
all the children who love stories
and the grandparents
who love to read to them.

READ TO ME
GRANDMA

pi kids® publications international, ltd.

Published by Louis Weber, C.E.O.
Publications International, Ltd.
7373 North Cicero Avenue, Lincolnwood, Illinois 60712
Ground Floor, 59 Gloucester Place, London W1U 8JJ

Customer Service: 1-800-595-8484 or customer_service@pilbooks.com

www.pilbooks.com

p i kids is a registered trademark of Publications International, Ltd.

Permission is never granted for commercial purposes.
Manufactured in China.

8 7 6 5 4 3 2 1

ISBN-13: 978-1-4127-6609-8
ISBN-10: 1-4127-6609-5

READ TO ME, GRANDMA
TABLE OF CONTENTS

Aladdin

Retold by Gayla Amaral

The Sultan's guard dashed through the city streets, screaming, "Stop, thief!"

"Hurry, Abu!" Aladdin shouted to his monkey as they ran through the market, leaping from roofs and carrying a stolen loaf of bread.

Aladdin was always in trouble. As a poor street boy, he lived by the saying "Gotta steal to eat."

But seeing two hungry children, kind Aladdin gave them his bread. He was not just a poor kid on the streets; he was a "diamond in the rough."

Meanwhile at his castle, the Sultan consulted Jafar about his daughter, Princess Jasmine.

"What can I do?" asked the Sultan. "Jasmine refuses to marry any of the princes I choose for her."

Jafar was the Sultan's trusted adviser. But the Sultan didn't know that he was also plotting to steal the throne.

"I can help," Jafar replied, "but I must have your ring."

Jafar needed the magic ring to find the one person who could enter the Cave of Wonders and steal its magic lamp. The person had to be a "diamond in the rough," and with the ring, Jafar discovered the "diamond" was Aladdin!

Elsewhere, Princess Jasmine was sitting by herself.

"If I can't marry for love," she said to her pet tiger, "then I don't want to be a princess!"

Before dawn the following morning, Jasmine sneaked outside the castle walls. She was amazed at the hustle and bustle of the marketplace. The minute Aladdin laid eyes on Jasmine, he knew that he had to meet her.

Jasmine told Aladdin she ran away because her father was forcing her to marry. Aladdin and Jasmine instantly became friends. After all, they both felt trapped by their circumstances.

Suddenly, Jafar's guards arrived. They captured Aladdin, and Jasmine threw off her cloak, revealing who she was.

"By order of the princess, let him go!" Jasmine demanded. The guards refused, so she hurried to the castle and demanded that Jafar release Aladdin. But Jafar lied to her, saying it was too late and that Aladdin was already gone.

While Jasmine cried, Aladdin sat in the dungeon thinking about her. Suddenly, an old prisoner approached Aladdin with a plan, saying, "I'll help you escape—if you bring me a lamp from the Cave of Wonders."

Aladdin accepted the old man's offer. Escaping, Aladdin and Abu traveled with the old man to the Cave of Wonders.

"Touch nothing but the lamp!" the Cave warned Aladdin.

Aladdin and Abu found the lamp with the help of a friendly Magic Carpet. Unfortunately, Abu touched the forbidden treasure, and the Cave began to crumble. The Magic Carpet rescued them and took them to the old man, who was really Jafar in disguise.

"Give me the lamp!" Jafar screamed, grabbing it and pushing Aladdin back into the Cave.

Outside the Cave of Wonders, Jafar cackled with glee, for he finally had the lamp. But crafty Abu had stolen the lamp from Jafar, and gave it to Aladdin!

Trapped in the Cave with Abu and the Magic Carpet, Aladdin examined the lamp.

"It looks like a piece of junk," he said curiously. "But I wonder what this writing means."

As Aladdin rubbed some dust off the lamp, a cloud of smoke poured out, revealing a giant blue genie!

"Master, I will grant you three wishes," the Genie told Aladdin.

Aladdin didn't want to use up his wishes, so he tricked the Genie into getting them out of the Cave of Wonders.

As soon as they had escaped, the Genie turned to Aladdin and asked, "Master, what is your first wish?"

"Can you make me a prince?" Aladdin asked.

Poof! At the Genie's command, Aladdin became Prince Ali Ababwa! Then the Genie turned Abu into an elephant who proudly carried the new prince into the palace courtyard.

When Aladdin asked Jasmine to marry him, she refused immediately. But after a moonlit carpet ride, Princess Jasmine realized that Prince Ali was actually her beloved Aladdin.

10

Meanwhile, Jafar still plotted to become Sultan. To do this, he planned to marry Jasmine and get rid of Aladdin. Stealing the lamp, Jafar made the Genie grant him two wishes — to be Sultan *and* the most powerful sorcerer.

"You're not as powerful as the Genie," said Aladdin, tricking Jafar into using his final wish.

"I wish to be a powerful Genie," Jafar said. But he forgot one detail — genies live inside lamps until they are rubbed.

Aladdin used his final wish to free his own Genie. Then the "diamond in the rough" married Princess Jasmine and they lived happily ever after!

The Incredibles

Retold by Leslie Lindecker

Mr. Incredible was a very busy Super. He had his hands full rescuing damsels in distress and catching villains. Our hero was preventing a thief named Bomb Voyage from robbing a bank when something strange happened: a boy named Buddy arrived to help him.

"Call me Incrediboy!" Buddy said. "I'm your biggest fan!"

"I can help you!" he added. "I invented rocket boots that help me fly. We can fight the bad guys together!"

"Go home, Buddy," Mr. Incredible said. "I work alone."

Buddy left, feeling sad that Mr. Incredible did not appreciate him. Sadly, many of the people Mr. Incredible and the other Supers helped did not appreciate *them*. The public complained about the broken windows, the smashed brick walls, and the uprooted trees.

Soon there was a public outcry against all Supers. Some people sued the Supers for the damage they had done. The city passed a ban that said Supers could not be heroes any longer. They could not battle villains or rescue people. The Supers had to go into hiding and live like normal people.

Mr. Incredible married Elastigirl, another Super. For normal names they chose Bob and Helen Parr. Bob worked for an insurance company, while Helen raised their three children, Violet, Dash, and Jack-Jack.

Things weren't always normal inside the Parr residence. Dash would run at super speeds through the house while Violet tried to stop him. Helen would use her Elastigirl arms to separate the two when they were fighting.

"Can't we just have a peaceful meal?" Bob would ask.

"Sometimes it's hard to be normal," Bob said one day.

"You should go bowling with Lucius," Helen said. "That's a normal thing to do."

"Good idea," Bob said. He called his friend Lucius, an ice-throwing Super named Frozone, to go bowling.

But instead of bowling, Bob and Lucius listened to police radios to see if there were any people they could save.

"A burning building!" Bob said. "We can rescue people!"

Mr. Incredible did not know that they were being watched.

One day, a mysterious woman named Mirage contacted Bob. "We know who you are and we need your help. We have an out-of-control robot that only you can stop," Mirage said.

Bob knew that Helen would not approve of this mission, so he told her that he was going on a business trip. As Mirage and Bob flew to the island of Nomanisan, she told him all about the dangerous robot, the Omnidroid 9000.

"It's a learning robot and we've lost control of it," Mirage told Bob. "You must stop it!"

Mirage and her boss, Syndrome, watched as Mr. Incredible tricked the robot into destroying itself.

After returning home, Bob tried to resume his normal life. But Mirage contacted him again. Bob went to a Super designer, Edna Mode, and had her make him a new costume, as his old one was ripped and ruined. Then he took Mirage's jet back to the island of Nomanisan.

When he arrived on the island, Mr. Incredible found a bigger, badder Omnidroid waiting for him! He fought it, but the robot quickly had the Super in its claws.

Mr. Incredible heard laughter. He turned around to find … "Buddy?" the surprised Super asked.

"Not anymore! The name is Syndrome now!" the villain cackled.

Back home, Helen found out all about Mirage and the evil robot. She knew that she had to rescue her poor husband. Having received new suits from Edna Mode for the entire family, Helen put on her new Elastigirl outfit and left the kids at home.

Helen borrowed a jet to take to Nomanisan. While flying over the ocean, she found that Violet and Dash had sneaked onto the jet. Now the entire Parr family was in danger!

Near the island, the jet was attacked by Syndrome's men. It was about to crash into the ocean! Thinking quickly, Helen turned herself into a parachute and the family floated down to the sea. In the water, Helen stretched into a boat and Dash motored them to the island.

Helen, Violet, and Dash sneaked into Syndrome's volcano fortress. Elastigirl found the computer banks that showed where Bob was being held. Violet and Dash distracted the guards while Helen helped her husband escape.

"We must stop Buddy, er, Syndrome!" said Bob. "He's going to use the robot to attack the city. Then he'll stop the robot and have himself declared a hero!"

"Not on my watch," said Helen.

"Let's get out of here!" Bob replied.

Helen and Bob
found Violet and Dash
outside fighting with
Syndrome's guards.
Syndrome ran up behind them
and caught the family in his immobi-ray.

"A whole family of Supers! How lucky I am!" said
Syndrome. "How sad that I must leave you now. I have to go
and save a city."

"I'm sorry I got you into this mess," Bob said to his family.

"I can get us out, Dad," said Violet, using her force-field
ability to break through the immobi-ray.

The Incredibles were back
in action!

"We must stop Syndrome,"
Bob said. "All of us!"

Taking one of Syndrome's rockets, the Incredibles were headed back to save the city from Syndrome and his robot.

Meanwhile, the Omnidroid had caused a lot of trouble and Syndrome was trying to realize his dreams of becoming a hero by stopping it. But the clever Omnidroid learned that Syndrome had a remote control and knocked it away.

Bob grabbed the robot's arm and turned it toward itself. Helen picked up the control and pushed the self-destruct button. The robot self-destructed and the city was saved!

"Three cheers for the Incredibles!" the crowd shouted.

The true Supers had won over evil and life was safe once again.

The Little Mermaid

Retold by Kate Hannigan

Once, in a kingdom beneath the sea, there lived a beautiful mermaid named Ariel. She was King Triton's youngest daughter and the best singer in the ocean. One day, her sisters performed a concert, singing in a fantastic show. But when the moment came for Ariel to appear, the stage was empty.

Ariel and her best friend, Flounder, were off exploring a sunken ship. Even though her father warned her about humans, Ariel loved to look for sunken human treasure.

She and Flounder discovered a fork and showed it to their friend Scuttle the seagull. "It's a dinglehopper!" Scuttle said. "Humans use these to brush their hair."

Suddenly, their adventures got a bit too exciting. "Shark!" screamed Flounder. Ariel looked up just in time to see a set of sharp white teeth snapping right before her eyes.

"Flounder, let's get out of here!" she yelled.

When Ariel returned home, King Triton was furious. "Where have you been?" he shouted.

Ariel was in deep trouble. Not only had she missed the concert, but Triton also found out Ariel had gone to the surface. He told her never to swim above the sea again.

Ariel cried and swam away to her favorite place: the cave where she hid her man-made treasures.

Gazing dreamily at a statue of dancers, she imagined what it would be like to have legs. She dreamed of leaving the mermaid world behind and living among humans.

At that instant, the ocean above Ariel grew dark. A ship was passing by!

Ariel raced to the surface and watched the humans aboard the ship. The moment she laid eyes on the dark-haired one called Prince Eric, Ariel was in love.

Just then a storm blew in, tossing the ship about. Ariel gasped as she saw Prince Eric fall into the sea.

"I must save him!" she cried.

Ariel pulled Eric through the churning water to the safety of the shore. She sang to him, and just as he awoke, she slipped back into the sea.

Ariel wanted to see Prince Eric again. But how?

The evil sea witch, Ursula, had a plan. If Ariel gave up her beautiful voice, Ursula would transform her into a human for three days. Then Ariel could be with Prince Eric.

"But the prince must kiss you by sunset on the third day," Ursula warned. "If he does, you'll remain human. If not, you will turn back into a mermaid and your soul will be mine!"

Ariel was ready. She began to sing, and Ursula greedily captured Ariel's angelic singing voice in a magic seashell.

In a flash, Ariel's mermaid tail split into two long legs. She swam to the surface of the water. She was a human!

Prince Eric was walking along the beach when he saw Ariel. "Could this be the one who rescued me?" he thought. But Eric remembered someone singing, and this girl couldn't speak.

Eric was confused. He brought Ariel back to his castle. She saw so many new and unusual things. But when Ariel spotted the dinglehopper, she knew just what to do. Ariel picked it up and began to brush her hair!

Ariel and Eric began to fall in love. But evil Ursula, disguised as a human named Vanessa, tricked them. At sunset on the third day, Ursula dragged Ariel to her lair.

"You're my prisoner now!" she shouted as Ariel turned back into a mermaid.

King Triton tried to rescue Ariel. Ursula offered to free her if the king would take Ariel's place. With Triton under her power, Ursula declared herself ruler of the sea.

Prince Eric knew Ariel and her father needed help. He fought Ursula in a fierce battle and destroyed her.

King Triton saw how much Ariel loved Eric. And he was grateful to Eric for saving the mermaid kingdom.

"I'm going to miss her," the king said. But he was not going to stand in true love's way.

With a wave of his powerful trident, the king transformed Ariel into a human again.

Ariel and Prince Eric were married that very day. And the mermaids and mermen of Triton's ocean kingdom swam to join the humans in celebration; their two worlds had at long last become one.

Monsters, Inc.

Retold by Guy Davis

Late one night, a bedroom closet slowly opened … and a creepy-crawly monster crept out! Terrified, a little boy sat up in bed and let out a scream so loud it woke up all of the neighbors.

The frightened boy ran down the hall and jumped into his parents' bed. Meanwhile, the creepy-crawly monster shut the door and scurried back to Monsters, Inc., where the other monsters congratulated him on a job well done.

"We scare because we care!" was the motto of Monsters, Inc., which powered the city of Monstropolis with the energy generated by screams. But not everything was perfect in Monstropolis. Kids today were becoming harder to scare, creating an energy shortage!

A monster named Sulley was the company's top scarer. He was helped by his best friend, Mike Wazowski. By scaring more children, they hoped to help with the energy crisis.

"Today's the day, Sulley!" said Mike, as they walked to work. "Today, we're going to set a new scare record!"

Almost everyone loved Sulley and Mike; they made a great team! But Randall, one of their coworkers, was jealous.

"I'll get more screams than you, Sulley," Randall hissed.

"May the best monster win!" said Sulley.

"I intend to," said Randall, turning away.

Even though it was a close race, Sulley beat Randall yet again. But after work, Sulley discovered that sneaky Randall was up to something. While snooping around, Randall had left one of the closet doors open, and a little girl walked through. Sulley hid the child in his bag so that Randall and the other monsters would not see her.

Only one thing scared the monsters of Monsters, Inc.—the touch of a human child! As their boss Waternoose always said, "There's nothing more toxic and deadly than a child!"

After Sulley placed the little girl in his bag, he raced to the famous Harryhausen's Restaurant and interrupted Mike's big date with his girlfriend, Celia.

"Sulley?" Mike asked, noticing his large friend. "What are you doing here?"

Before Sulley could answer, the little girl popped out of the bag and yelled, "Boo!"

The little girl's presence sent the entire city into a panic! Sulley and Mike were able to hide the girl from the authorities and race back to their apartment. They would get in trouble if anyone found out they had a child with them.

A petrified Mike tried to think of what to do with "Boo." But, as Sulley watched her play, he began to realize that she wasn't dangerous.

"Ya-ya-ya! Kitty!" giggled Boo.

As Boo laughed, the power surged. This meant that kids' laughter provided even more energy than their screams did.

"Mike, I don't think Boo is dangerous," said Sulley. "Can we keep her?"

Sulley and Mike decided to disguise Boo as a little monster and take her back to the factory.

"Don't worry, Boo," smiled Sulley. "We'll take you home."

At the factory, Sulley and Mike walked in on Randall and Waternoose working on a secret Scream Extractor … and they wanted to test it on Boo!

"I'm sorry about this, boys," said Waternoose.

"Sir, we just want to take Boo home," replied Sulley.

"Too late for that!" Waternoose said. "She's seen far too much!"

"I'll do anything to keep this company from going under!" shouted Waternoose. "Randall, get that little girl!"

Sulley and Mike knew there was only one thing left to do.

"If we can find Boo's door, we can get her home where she belongs," said Sulley. He and Mike raced into the factory and grabbed a closet door speeding along the production line.

"Hold on!" cried Sulley, jumping from one door to the next.

"Hurry!" yelled Mike. "Randall's right behind us!"

At last, Sulley and Mike found Boo's closet door.

As Sulley and Mike returned Boo to her bedroom, Randall and Waternoose were quickly taken away by the authorities.

Suddenly, Sulley had a great idea to solve the energy crisis. "A child's laughter is ten times more powerful than a child's screams!" he said as the employees cheered. "We'll use laughs instead of screams. Monsters, Inc. is back in business!"

As for Boo? Every night, she gets a good-night hug from her two favorite monsters.

Beauty and the Beast

Retold by Kate Hannigan

Once upon a time in a sleepy village, there lived a beautiful girl named Belle. She liked to read books about exciting and faraway lands. These places were different from her town, where everything was always the same.

"Give that back," Belle said to Gaston, the town bully, as he snatched a book from her. He wanted to marry Belle, but she had dreams of her own.

Belle lived with her papa, whom she loved with all her heart. One day Papa rode off to the fair on his horse, Phillipe.

Before long, Phillipe returned home, but Papa was missing. Belle knew Papa must be in trouble. She jumped on Phillipe's back, and the horse took her to a gloomy castle. There she found Papa, locked in a dungeon!

Suddenly, a Beast appeared. "This is my castle!" he roared. "Let my father go," Belle pleaded. "I'll stay in his place."

Belle was happy Papa was free, but now she was a prisoner in the Beast's castle forever. Whom would she talk to? Who would be her friends?

"I thought you might like a spot of tea," said a voice. Belle looked up and saw that a teapot was talking to her. "Hello, my name is Mrs. Potts," said the friendly teapot.

A clock, a teacup, and a feather duster were smiling at her, too. The castle was enchanted! Belle was delighted. With friends like these, she would never be lonely.

"Let me show you around the place," Cogsworth the clock said, bowing politely.

40

The whole castle was Belle's to explore—everywhere except the West Wing. But her curiosity was too great, and Belle sneaked into the forbidden room. A beautiful red rose encased in glass caught her eye. She reached out to touch it.

"I told you not to come here!" shouted the Beast.

Belle didn't know that the rose was part of a terrible spell. If the Beast could learn to love and be loved in return before its last petal fell, the spell would be broken. If not, he would remain a Beast forever.

The Beast's anger frightened Belle. She ran from the room and straight to the front door. She wanted to go home!

The Beast let Belle go. But as she made her way through the dark woods, a pack of growling wolves attacked.

Suddenly, the Beast appeared and bravely fought off the wolves. "Leave her alone!" he shouted. The wolves were scared and ran back into the woods.

The Beast saved Belle's life, but the fight left him badly hurt.

Belle took the Beast to his castle and looked at his wounds. "I'll take care of you," she said and nursed him back to health.

Belle was grateful to the Beast for saving her. She saw that despite his unpleasant ways, the Beast was kind inside.

The Beast was growing to trust Belle, too. They began to spend their days together, taking long walks, feeding birds, and reading stories. One night they danced together—just like a prince and a princess.

Belle was no longer afraid of the Beast, but the villagers were. Gaston led them to the Beast's castle. He wanted to destroy the Beast and make Belle his wife.

Gaston and the Beast battled as a storm crashed around them. Fighting, they climbed the tallest tower of the castle. Gaston slipped in the rain, fell, and was gone—but not before he wounded the Beast.

Belle cried out as the Beast roared in pain. "Please, don't leave me," Belle said. "I love you."

Belle's tears fell onto the Beast. She thought she'd lost him. But he was still alive and her love had broken the spell!

Belle gasped as a flash of light surrounded them. She watched as the Beast was transformed into a handsome prince. All the enchanted servants in the castle became human again, too.

"Hooray!" cheered Mrs. Potts and the others.

Belle and the Prince were to be married. And when Belle slipped her hand into the Prince's and began to dance, it was just the beginning of their happily ever after.

Toy Story

Retold by Guy Davis

Today was Andy's birthday—but not everyone was happy. Andy's toys were nervous that they'd be replaced by the new toys he received as gifts.

"Calm down, everyone," said Woody. "No one is getting replaced!"

"That's easy for you to say," cried Rex nervously. "You're Andy's favorite!"

It was true — Woody had been Andy's favorite toy for years. That's why everyone was surprised when it seemed that Woody was being replaced by a new toy!

Andy came to his bedroom with the new toy, a space ranger named Buzz Lightyear.

After Andy left, Buzz looked at his new surroundings.

"Buzz Lightyear to Star Command," said the space ranger. "My ship has run off course. There seems to be no sign of intelligent life anywhere."

Just then, Buzz spotted Woody. "I am Buzz Lightyear," he announced. "I come in peace."

"Howdy, Buzz," replied Woody. "There's a little problem. I'm Andy's favorite toy, and Andy's bed is my space."

But Buzz never got a chance to answer Woody as he was suddenly surrounded by the other toys.

"What exactly does a space ranger do?" asked Slinky.

"Can you fly?" asked Hamm.

Woody was jealous that the other toys were so impressed.

"Of course he can't fly!" cried Woody. "He is a TOY!"

"You are a sad, strange little man," Buzz said to Woody. To the others, he said, "I *can* fly — to infinity and beyond!"

Buzz jumped off the bed onto a ball and back onto the bed.

"That's just falling … with style," grumbled poor Woody.

Later,
Andy's family was
headed to Pizza Planet. Woody
had come up with a plan to get rid of Buzz.

"Hey Buzz," said Woody, "at Pizza Planet, there are
spaceships! We can transport you home!"

"Good idea!" said Buzz. The two hid in the family car.

At Pizza Planet, Buzz and Woody lost Andy. Soon, they
were trapped in an arcade game and surrounded by aliens.

Unfortunately, Sid, Andy's toy-torturing neighbor,
happened to be at Pizza Planet, too. "Let's play!" he said.

Evil Sid took Buzz and Woody home. Sid put them with his other mutilated toys. Woody didn't know which was worse: waiting to be tortured by Sid or watching Sid's sister humiliate Buzz by dressing him up in a pretty pink outfit.

"One minute you're defending the galaxy, the next you're having tea as Mrs. Nesbit," said Buzz sadly, waving his broken arm around. "You're right, Woody. I'm just a silly toy."

"Buzz, there's no time to feel sorry for yourself!" said Woody. "We need to get home! Andy's family is moving to another city tomorrow!"

Sid came back to his room and tied Buzz to a rocket. Woody knew he had to act fast.

"Your toys see everything, Sid," said Woody, acting a little scary and blowing out Sid's match. "So … play nice!"

Sid ran from his room, screaming, "The toys are alive!"

"Snap out of it!" Woody told Buzz. "You're Buzz Lightyear! You glow in the dark! You've got wings! You're cool!" He continued, "More importantly, Andy needs us, and we need to work together to get out of here!"

"You're
right!" cried Buzz.
"We need to get on that moving van!"

But as they ran out of Sid's house, the van was leaving.

Buzz and Woody spotted RC, a speedy toy race car.

Jumping on RC, Woody lit the rocket strapped to Buzz's back.

Suddenly, all three toys were rocketing down the street.

"Buzz!" shouted Woody. "You're flying!"

"This isn't flying," cried Buzz. "It's falling… with style!"

Woody shouted, "To infinity … and beyond!"

"Watch out! We're going to miss the van!" cried Woody.

"We're not aiming for the van," shouted Buzz. "We're aiming for Andy's car!"

Using his wings to glide, Buzz let the rocket fly off before it exploded. Then, they flew right through the car's sunroof and plopped down next to Andy.

"Woody! Buzz!" cried Andy, picking up the toys. "Look, mom—I found them!"

"I knew they'd turn up," said Andy's mom.

As Andy hugged his two favorite toys, Woody gave Buzz a wink. The rivals had become friends at last!

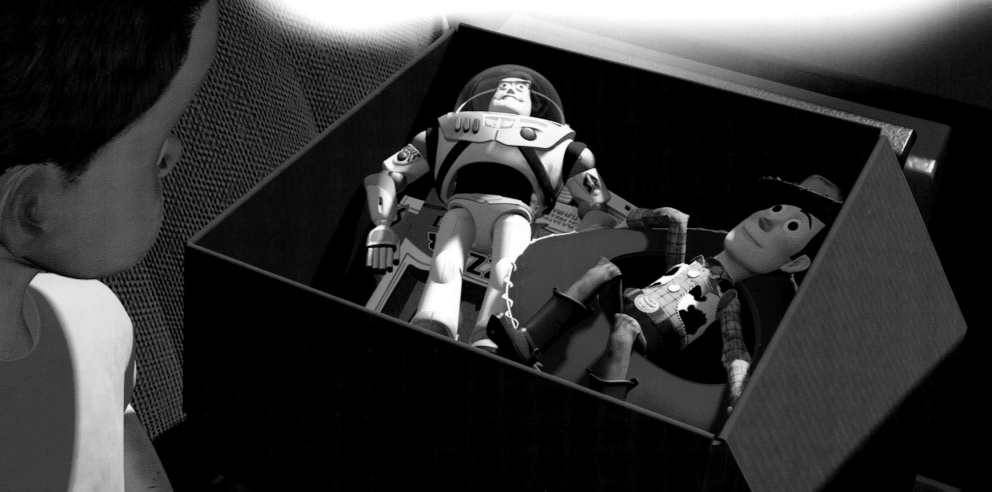

The Lion King

Retold by Gayla Amaral

Mufasa stood atop Pride Rock. The beloved king of the Pride Lands was especially happy as he observed his kingdom with his son, Simba.

"Look, Simba, as far as the light shines," Mufasa said. "When you are king, this will be your kingdom."

"It's all mine?" exclaimed Simba. "Wow!"

"Yes, everything except the elephant graveyard," warned Mufasa. "You must promise never to go there!"

As Simba gazed out over the kingdom, he saw elephants, giraffes, monkeys, zebras, and many more animals bowing before him. Simba couldn't wait to be king!

Everyone was thrilled with the young prince—everyone except Scar. Scar was Mufasa's brother. He had always been jealous of Mufasa, and now he was jealous of Simba, too.

"Life is not fair," growled Scar. "*I* should be the king!"

So Scar plotted to get rid of Simba by slyly convincing the young lion to visit the elephant graveyard.

And Simba fell for Scar's evil trick.

Simba hurried to find his best friend, Nala. "Come with me," urged Simba. "I heard about a really cool place."

As Simba and Nala entered the spooky graveyard, they were both frightened. Soon they were surrounded by a pack of laughing hyenas. As the hyenas closed in on them, Mufasa pounced into the fray and rescued the young lions!

"Being brave doesn't mean you go looking for trouble," lectured Mufasa. Simba felt bad that he had disappointed his father and put Nala in danger.

Even though Simba was safe, Scar wasn't giving up on his plan to be king. He convinced the evil hyenas to help him.

"Run into the herd of wildebeests and cause them to stampede," Scar told them. The hyenas did as he said, and poor Simba was caught in the stampede. And just as he had before, the brave Mufasa rescued his son.

As Mufasa struggled and tried to climb to safety, he cried out to Scar, "Brother, please help me!"

But Scar refused, and Mufasa fell, disappearing from sight.

Simba blamed himself for the
loss of Mufasa, and Scar shamed him into running away.
Traveling far away, Simba met two new friends — Timon, a
funny meerkat, and Pumbaa, a warmhearted warthog.

"Don't be sad," said Timon. "Our motto is *hakuna matata.*"

Simba had no idea what those words meant, so Pumbaa
explained, "*Hakuna matata* means 'no worries.'"

Soon Simba adopted this no-worries lifestyle. But even
though his new life was carefree, Simba missed his family.

Before long, Simba grew from a cub into a handsome lion.
One day, a lioness suddenly appeared and began to chase
poor Pumbaa. Quickly coming to his friend's rescue, Simba
found himself face-to-face with Nala. Simba couldn't believe
his eyes. It was his best friend from the Pride Lands!

"What are you doing?" asked Simba in disbelief.

"I'm hunting," Nala replied. "Pride Rock has no water or
food. Please come home. You're our king and our only hope!"

But Simba refused to go until
Rafiki, a wise old baboon,
reminded him that he must
be true to his destiny.

Together, the four friends
returned to Pride Rock. Scar had been
a terrible king, and Simba was shocked at
the horrible condition of the kingdom.

To take his rightful place as king, Simba knew he must
challenge Scar. While his friends distracted the hyenas,
Simba ordered Scar to step down from his throne.

"Run away, Scar," roared Simba, "and never return!"

As he leaped to attack Simba, Scar fell off the cliff and
landed far below among the howling pack of hungry hyenas.

All of the animals in the Pride Lands celebrated the homecoming of King Simba! Simba was grateful to Timon and Pumbaa for their help, and he was grateful to Rafiki for reminding him of his responsibility.

Soon the kingdom was restored to its natural beauty. Simba and Nala were overjoyed to spend their lives together and became the proud parents of their own baby lion cub.

As Simba stood proudly on Pride Rock, he was thankful that he, his father, and his daughter were all a part of the Circle of Life!

Finding Nemo

Retold by Guy Davis

Nemo tried to hurry his father along. "It's the first day of school!" he called energetically.

As the two orange clown fish swam toward the school on the coral reef, Marlin looked at his son.

"Are you sure you're ready to go to school this year, son?" Marlin asked nervously.

"Because you could always wait five or six years…."

"No, Dad," said Nemo, rolling his eyes. "I'm ready! I'm ready!"

"Just remember, Nemo," said Marlin, "stay close to the other fish. The ocean's not safe."

Later, Nemo and his new schoolmates wandered away from their teacher. On a dare to touch a boat, the little clown fish swam into open waters—right into a scuba diver!

"Dad! Help!" cried Nemo, as he was swept up into the diver's net.

"Nemo!" shouted Marlin, who was swimming nearby. He frantically swam after the diver's boat. But it was too late. Nemo was gone!

63

Marlin swam
up to a group of fish.
He cried, "I've lost my son!
He was taken by a boat!"

"A boat?" replied Dory, a
blue tang. "I'm Dory. I can help.
I just saw a boat! Follow me!"

Marlin swam after Dory as fast
as he could. Suddenly, Dory stopped.

"Stop following me!" Dory yelled.

"You said you would help me!" said Marlin.

"Oh, I did?" replied a sheepish Dory. "I'm sorry. I suffer
from short-term memory loss."

"You're wasting my time!" said Marlin angrily.

"Mr. Grumpy-Gills, do you know what you gotta do when life gets you down?" asked Dory. "Just keep swimming . . . ."

Then, Marlin and Dory realized they were swimming with sharks! But these weren't regular sharks—they wanted to stop eating fish. Their motto was "Fish are friends, not food!"

Swimming away, Marlin spotted the diver's mask.

"It's from Sydney, Australia," said Dory, reading the address on the mask. "That must be where Nemo is!"

Far away in Sydney, Nemo was in an aquarium in a dentist's office. The dentist was the diver who had captured him.

A friendly pelican named Nigel stuck his head in the window to say hello to his fish friends.

"Who's the new kid?" Nigel asked.

"His name is Nemo," replied Gill, the leader of the fish.

"You're Nemo?" asked Nigel. "I've heard of you! Your dad has been searching the whole ocean for you! He's even taken on sharks! He'll stop at nothing until he finds you!"

Meanwhile, Marlin was
desperately trying to find
Sydney, Australia.

"It's no use," he said. "No fish
in the ocean can help me."

"I'm helping," said Dory.

Just then, the two found themselves surrounded by jellyfish.

"Stay away from their tentacles!" said Marlin. "They sting!"

It was too late—Dory had been stung! "Hold on," said

Marlin bravely. "I'll get us out of here!"

Grabbing his friend, Marlin swam until they were safe.

Back at his office, the dentist
was planning to give Nemo to
his obnoxious niece, Darla.
"I'm a piranha!" the girl snapped.
Thinking quickly, Nemo closed his eyes
and floated upside down. He pretended to be dead
so the dentist would flush him down the drain.
"Great idea!" cried Gill. "All drains lead to the ocean!"
Sure enough, Nemo was able to escape down the sink.

Nemo found himself carried down one pipe after another. Finally, he reached his destination—Sydney Harbor!

Meanwhile, Marlin and Dory had hitched a ride with a whale. As they entered Sydney Harbor, the whale blasted the two little fish out of his spout. "We made it!" said Marlin.

Finally, after a little more searching, Nemo and Marlin found each other in Sydney Harbor and headed back home together.

"I love you, Dad," said Nemo.

"I love you, too, son," smiled Marlin.

A Bug's Life

Retold by Leslie Lindecker

It was an ant's way of life. Gather the food, store the food, eat the food. Flik knew he could come up with a better way to do things. He wanted to tell Princess Atta.

"Let me show you my new invention," Flik said.

"Why aren't you in line with the other ants?" Atta asked.

Queen and Dot, Atta's mother and sister, laughed at Flik.

"It's a harvesting machine," Flik explained. "It will help us gather food much faster."

Atta said, "Now we must gather food for the grasshoppers or they will be angry. Please get in line with the other ants. Take your food to the gathering place. We must hurry."

Flik took the grain he had gathered in his machine up to the gathering place. He tipped the grain onto the pile.

As Flik took off his harvesting machine, he bumped into the stack of grain.

He watched in horror as the entire pile tumbled into the creek.

Just as Flik returned to the anthill to tell Princess Atta what happened, they heard a loud whirring overhead.

"The grasshoppers," the ants whispered nervously.

The grasshoppers punched their way down into the anthill and swarmed around the frightened ants.

"Where is our food?" demanded Hopper, the biggest, meanest grasshopper.

"Sir, there was an accident," Flik began.

"There is no food?" yelled Hopper. "We will be back! You must gather more food for us!"

Flik felt terrible. It was all his fault. He had tipped the food into the creek. But he suddenly came up with a great idea.

"Princess Atta, we should fight the grasshoppers!" he said. "But we'll need bigger bugs to help us."

"There are no bigger bugs here, Flik," Atta said.

"I will find some and bring them back with me," Flik vowed. He set off for the City to find some larger friends.

When Flik got to the City, he met some very interesting bugs. They told him stories of their daring acts.

"You must be great warriors!" Flik exclaimed.

"Ah, yes!" said one bug.

"But of course!" said another bug.

The bugs did not tell Flik that they weren't warriors. They were really just a group of out-of-work flea circus bugs.

"I need your help," Flik said. He told the bugs about the grasshoppers. The bugs agreed to help Flik and the ants.

"Hop on," said the largest bug, lifting everyone off the ground with a great buzzing of wings. And off the bugs flew, back to the anthill.

Princess Atta, Dot, Queen, and the ants were amazed to see Flik return with his warrior bugs. Now they needed a plan.

"What will scare the grasshoppers away?" Flik asked.

"A big bird!" said Princess Atta. "But it would eat us, too."

Flik said, "We could build a bird that we could fly from the inside. It would scare the grasshoppers away forever."

So the ants and the warrior bugs built a big bird of twigs and leaves. They hauled it up into a tree and fastened it with a long vine.

The ants were
ready when the
grasshoppers returned.
The circus bugs put on a show and
dazzled Hopper and the other grasshoppers. Meanwhile, Flik
ran up to the bird and climbed inside. The ants held the vine
and pushed the bird.

Suddenly, Flik's contraption swooped down at Hopper.
"A bird! Run for your lives!" he yelled.
The ants ran behind them, making bird noises.

The other grasshoppers saw and heard all
of this and scattered everywhere.
The ants cheered. They were free
at last. The grasshoppers were gone!

Princess Atta took Flik's hand. "You did it! You saved us from the grasshoppers."

"*We* did it," Flik said. "We make a great team."

"And you will make a great queen," Queen said to Atta. She placed her crown atop Atta's head.

The warrior bugs gathered by Flik. "We must go now, but we have a great story to tell: the story of Flik," said one bug.

"And his big bird of twigs and leaves," added another.

The ants waved to the warrior bugs as they left, happy that they could live in peace.

Lilo & Stitch

Retold by Gayla Amaral

Splash! Lilo jumped into the ocean. She knew she would be late to her hula dance class, a very important class for young girls in the Hawaiian islands. But she just had to feed her pet fish! After all, the fish were her only friends. No one else ever wanted to play with her.

So Lilo ran to class dripping wet. Once again, she was in big trouble.

After class, Lilo was supposed to wait for her sister, Nani, who had taken care of her since they had become orphans. But when the other girls wouldn't let Lilo play, she ran home crying. Lilo locked the door, threw herself onto the floor, and turned up her Elvis Presley record full blast.

"I get so lonely … ," sang Elvis as "Heartbreak Hotel" blared from the speakers.

Lilo knew exactly how it felt to be lonely. Suddenly, she heard Nani banging on the locked door.

"Let me in, Lilo!" Nani yelled. "The social worker is coming today!"

When the social worker, Mr. Bubbles, arrived, he angrily looked around the house. Nani hoped that Lilo would behave. Nani loved her sister, but sometimes Lilo drove her crazy. And it didn't help that the house was messy.

To make matters worse, Lilo complained that she was mistreated. "Call if you ever need me," Mr. Bubbles told Lilo.

Even though Nani was angry, she reassured Lilo that they were a family. Later that night, they saw a falling star in the night sky, and Lilo made a wish.

"I want someone to be my friend," Lilo wished.

But it wasn't a falling star that they saw. Instead, it was an alien spaceship that crashed on another part of the island. Inside was an alien called Experiment 626 that had come from another planet. Jumba Jukiba, an evil scientist, had created Experiment 626 to destroy everything in its path, but it had escaped and landed on Earth.

While exploring, Experiment 626 was hit by a truck. The truckers thought the strange creature looked a little like a dog, so they took it to an animal shelter.

The next day, Lilo and Nani arrived at the animal shelter to find a pet. Nani thought that a dog would keep Lilo from being so lonely.

"I want that dog," said Lilo, pointing to Experiment 626. "And I think I'll name him Stitch!"

Nani thought that Stitch was the strangest

dog she had ever seen, but Lilo liked him and couldn't wait to show Stitch around the island.

They went on a picnic, played at the beach, ate snow cones, and went to a luau. But no matter what they did, wild little Stitch destroyed everything that he touched.

Nani was afraid that Mr. Bubbles was going to take Lilo to a new home, so that night she hugged Lilo and sang her their favorite Hawaiian song. No matter what, they were still family.

Lilo wanted Stitch to be part of the family, too. Lilo was sure he felt lost without a family—just like she had felt.

"*Ohana* means family," Lilo said. "And that means nobody gets left behind."

Even though Stitch finally understood about family, he thought Lilo would be better off without him and ran away that night.

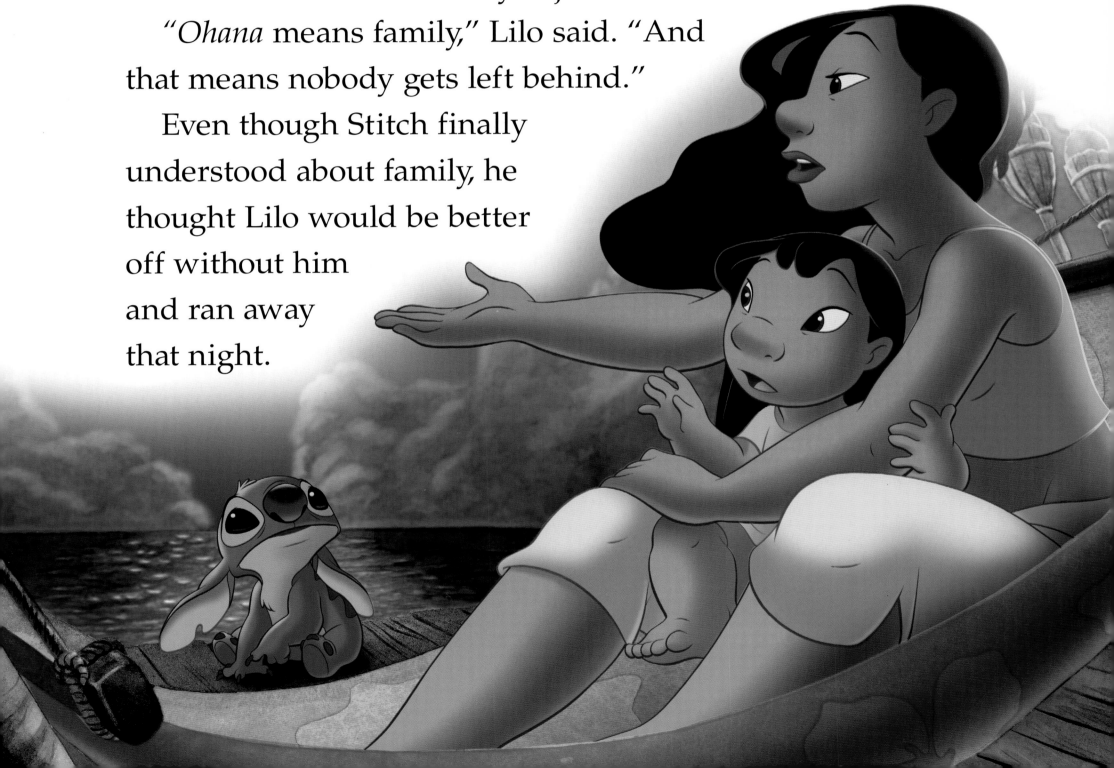

"There you are!" Jumba shouted when he discovered Stitch hiding in the forest. Jumba and Agent Pleakley had come to Earth in order to take Stitch back to their planet, Turo.

Stitch explained to them that he was looking for his family.

"You don't have a family," growled Jumba. "You can never belong!"

But Stitch knew he belonged with Lilo. She wanted to be his family!

After a wild chase around the island, Stitch ran home to Lilo with Jumba and Agent Pleakley close on his heels.

"This is my family," Stitch told Jumba and Agent Pleakley. "I found them on my own!"

Lilo hugged Stitch. "It's a little family," she said, "but it's still good!"

Jumba and Agent Pleakley were so touched that Stitch had found a family that they stopped chasing him. Even Mr. Bubbles agreed that this strange group was a good family.

Later, as they played on the beach, Lilo looked around at Nani and Stitch. They made a strange family, indeed … but they were her family and she loved them!

Toy Story 2

Retold by Kate Hannigan

Woody was a cowboy doll who belonged to a boy named Andy. He was Andy's favorite toy. One day Andy went to summer camp and left Woody behind.

After Andy left, Woody sat on a shelf in Andy's room and watched Andy's mom collect toys for a yard sale.

"Don't sell Wheezy," thought Woody as Andy's mom picked up his penguin friend. "I've got to save him!"

Before he knew it, Woody accidentally wound up in the yard sale, too—in a box of toys for sale.

"How much for the cowboy doll?" asked a man at the yard sale. He was excited to buy Woody.

Andy's mom was surprised to see Andy's favorite toy outside. She wondered how he had been mixed in with the toys she was selling. "He's not for sale," she said.

The man didn't care. He waited until Andy's mom wasn't looking and snatched Woody. He jumped into his car and sped off with the stolen cowboy doll.

Woody's friend Buzz Lightyear was watching from the window upstairs. He chased after the car, but it got away.

Who would take Woody? The only clues were a white feather and the car's license-plate number—LZTYBRN.

That night in Andy's bedroom, Buzz and the other toys called a meeting. They had to solve this mystery and find Woody.

Suddenly, Buzz had an idea. The license plate spelled out Al's Toy Barn! They had just seen a TV commercial for Al's store. And in it, Al was dressed up in a white, feathery chicken suit.

That was it: Al had stolen Woody!

Buzz, Hamm, Mr. Potato Head, and Rex sprang into action. With Slinky Dog's help, they sneaked out of Andy's bedroom.

"To Al's Toy Barn and beyond!" Buzz Lightyear shouted.

But Woody wasn't at the toy store. Instead, Al had stashed the doll in his apartment.

"It's Woody!" whooped a cowgirl doll.

Woody was shocked. How did this doll know his name?

"Everybody knows your name," said Jessie, the cowgirl. She showed Woody an old TV show. He was the star! And Jessie, the Prospector, and a horse named Bullseye were his friends. They were called the Roundup gang.

Now that Al had found all four of them, he wanted to sell the gang to a toy museum in Japan.

Woody would never see Andy again!

Woody was sad. He told Jessie he belonged to Andy. "I'm his favorite toy," Woody said. "I can't go to Japan. I'd miss him."

Jessie remembered when she used to be somebody's favorite toy. She belonged to a little girl named Emily who loved her very much. Emily used to play with Jessie every day. But then she grew tired of Jessie and gave her away.

"You never forget kids like Emily or Andy," Jessie said. "But they forget you."

Woody didn't know what to do. Was Andy going to forget about him, too?

Back at Al's Toy Barn, Buzz Lightyear and the others were searching the store for Woody.

BEEP! BEEP! Mr. Potato Head and Hamm zoomed down the store's aisles in a plastic bus. "I thought we could ride in style," said Hamm.

Meanwhile, Rex sat in back of the bus and read a book about Buzz's enemy, Emperor Zurg.

Buzz walked up and down the rows.

Suddenly he came across an aisle with hundreds of other space rangers just like himself. Each doll looked exactly the same—like Buzz!

"Maybe I'm not such a special hero after all," Buzz thought to himself.

Buzz and the toys soon learned that Woody was at Al's apartment. As they raced from the toy store, another toy was secretly following them. It was Buzz's dreaded enemy, Emperor Zurg!

When the toys found Woody, he didn't want to go with them. He worried that Andy would not love him forever. Then he told them about the toy museum in Japan. "I'm a rare collectible doll," Woody bragged.

Buzz was shocked. "You are a *toy!*" Buzz said. "All that matters is if you're loved by a kid."

At the last minute, Woody said he wanted to go home after all. And he wanted his new friends to come, too.

Suddenly, Al returned! He put Woody and the Roundup gang into suitcases and left for the airport.

Buzz, Hamm, Rex, Mr. Potato Head, and Slinky ran for the elevator shaft. They had to get Woody out of Al's suitcase.

But Zurg was waiting for them.

"At last we meet again, Buzz Lightyear," Zurg said.

Buzz battled Zurg and saved his friends. Now he just had to save Woody!

When they reached the
airport, Buzz spotted one of
Al's suitcases. He popped open
the lid. Woody was inside!
"We've got to rescue
Jessie, too," shouted
Woody. He whistled for
Bullseye, and he and
Buzz jumped onto the
horse's back. "Ride
like the wind!"
Woody shouted.
Woody jumped
aboard the airplane
and found Jessie. But
the plane's wheels began to turn. They were taking off!
Just then Buzz rode to the rescue. He saved Woody and
Jessie—he *was* a special hero after all!

At home in Andy's room, Jessie worried that nobody would want her. Woody promised her that Andy's little sister would.

"A sister?" asked Jessie. "Why didn't you say that before?"

Woody told Buzz he wasn't worried that Andy would grow tired of him someday. "I'll always have you to keep me company," he said, "for infinity and beyond."

Finally the door opened, and in walked Andy. He was home from camp and happy to discover Jessie and Bullseye.

But best of all, Buzz Lightyear and his favorite toy, Woody, were there waiting to play.